Printed in the U.S.A.

ISBN 0-7172-8299-6

JIM HENSON'S MUPPETS
IN

Fozzie's Last Lap

A Book About Not Giving Up

By Richard Chevat • Illustrated by Joel Schick

GROLIER

Fozzie loved to swim. Actually, Fozzie loved to float. He was a great floater. He loved to lie back in the water and daydream and think of new jokes.

In the spring and summer, Fozzie went to the town pool almost every day. One day, as Fozzie was floating peacefully, a couple of kids swam by and splashed water all over him.

"Hey!" Fozzie yelled. "Watch out!"

"Sorry," said one of the kids. "We're practicing for the swim team tryouts. You can't get to be a fast swimmer if you don't practice."

"Swim team?" Fozzie said to himself as the two kids swam off. "That sounds like fun. Maybe I should try out, too."

Fozzie climbed out of the pool and found Mr. Dribble, the swim team coach.

"Sure, you can try out for the team," Mr. Dribble told him. "You have to be able to swim four laps in two minutes."

"Four laps?" Fozzie said, getting worried. "I've never even swum *two* laps. Isn't there a team for floaters?"

"I'm afraid not," Mr. Dribble answered. "But why don't you try out, anyway? Go ahead. I'll time you."

Fozzie went to one end of the pool and jumped in. He felt nervous as the coach took out his stopwatch.

Mr. Dribble said, "Ready? Set? Go!"

Fozzie swam toward the far end of the pool with all his might. He finished the first lap with no trouble. He turned and headed back. He finished the second lap. Now he was getting tired.

"You're doing great, Fozzie!" Mr. Dribble called out to him.

After the third lap, Fozzie's arms and legs were aching. His lungs felt like they were going to burst. The other end of the pool looked like it was a mile away.

"I can't do it," he said, and hung onto the side of the pool.

"Too bad," Mr. Dribble said. "You gave it a good try, and you only had one more lap to go. But there are still two weeks till swim season starts. Maybe if you practice hard, you'll still be able to make the team."

"Practice?" Fozzie said to himself. It sounded like a lot of work.

Fozzie went home, and that night when he fell asleep, he was still thinking about the swim team. As he slept, he had a dream that he was a world championship swimmer. He was so fast that he raced through the water like a dolphin. He finished the last lap of a big race before the other swimmers had even started!

The next morning, he jumped out of bed bright and early.

"I can do it!" he said. "I'm going to make the swim team, no matter what!"

So Fozzie started to practice his swimming. Every day, he went down to the pool and practiced swimming laps. Coach Dribble gave him pointers on how to improve his stroke. Each day, he swam a little stronger and a little faster.

At the end of the first week, Coach Dribble timed Fozzie while he tried to swim the four laps again.

One lap...two laps...three laps. Fozzie swam back down the pool for the last lap. But halfway there, he got out of breath and had to stop.

"I...still...can't...do it," he gasped, as he hung onto the side of the pool.

"There's still one more week," Coach Dribble said encouragingly. "You're getting better all the time. Keep practicing."

"I will," Fozzie said. "I'll keep trying."

And he kept on practicing. On Saturday, he rode his bike with Kermit and Piggy, but as soon as they got home, he dashed to the pool to practice some more.

On Sunday morning, Fozzie's dad found him practicing his stroke right in the middle of his bed.

Fozzie practiced whenever he could. When he wasn't in the pool, he *imagined* practicing—even while he was eating supper.

By Friday, Fozzie had improved so much that he could finish all four laps. But he still couldn't do them in two minutes.

"Tomorrow's the last day for tryouts," Coach Dribble told him. "If you don't make the team this year, you can try again next year."

"No," said Fozzie. "I've gone this far. I'm not going to give up. I'll be back tomorrow."

The next day, Fozzie went back to the pool for his last try. Kermit, Piggy, and Scooter went with him to cheer him on.

"Good luck, Fozzie," Kermit said. "I know you can do it."

"Uh, thanks," said Fozzie. But deep
down, he wasn't so sure.

"Ready, Fozzie?" Coach Dribble asked.
Fozzie nodded and got into the pool. "Go!"
shouted the coach, and Fozzie pushed off
with a mighty kick.

"Go, Fozzie!" shouted Piggy, Kermit, and Scooter.

Fozzie was swimming as fast as he could. He finished the first lap.

I'm going to do it, he thought to himself as he made his first turn.

"Wocka! Wocka!" Kermit yelled, trying to say it the way Fozzie always did.

Fozzie finished the second lap. *I'm going to do it,* he thought.

"He's right on time," Coach Dribble said to Fozzie's friends, looking at the stopwatch. "But he's slowing down."

By the time Fozzie had finished the third lap, his arms and legs were aching. He was gasping for breath. But he kept swimming as hard as he could.

I can do it! he thought to himself, and
tried to swim even faster.

"He's going to make it!" Kermit shouted.

"Come on, Fozzie!" screamed Piggy.

I'm going to do it! Fozzie thought as he
took one last stroke and reached for the end
of the pool.

'That's it!" Coach Dribble cried, looking at his watch. "You did it!"

Fozzie hung onto the edge of the pool with a big, tired grin on his face.

"I did it," he said. "I made the team."

"You sure did!" Kermit shouted excitedly as he ran over to congratulate his friend. "Way to go, Fozzie!"

"You hung on and didn't quit," Coach Dribble said. "Fozzie, I'm proud of you."

"Let's go get some ice cream!" shouted Kermit. "Three scoops for Fozzie!"

"Do you think you can eat three scoops, Fozzie?" asked Scooter.

"I never did before," said Fozzie with a smile. "But it'll sure be fun to practice."

Let's Talk About Not Giving Up

Sometimes, when things are hard to do, it can seem a lot easier to just give up. Fozzie felt that way about the swimming tryouts for awhile, but he kept trying. And when he finally passed the test for the swim team, it made him feel really terrific! But even if Fozzie hadn't made the team, he would have been a winner because he'd tried his best.

Here are some questions about not giving up for you to think about:

Did you ever have to do something really hard, and you kept at it until you got it right?

What helped you keep trying?

How did you feel when you were done?